MARY-KATE & ASHLEY

Starring in

WHEN IN ROME™

A novelization by Megan Stine

Based on the teleplay by Michael Swerdlick

▟HarperEntertainment
An Imprint of HarperCollins*Publishers*

A PARACHUTE PRESS BOOK

PARACHUTE PRESS

Parachute Publishing, L.L.C.
156 Fifth Avenue
New York, NY 10010

 **DUALSTAR PUBLICATIONS**

Dualstar Publications
c/o Thorne and Company
1801 Century Park East
Los Angeles, CA 90067

HarperEntertainment

An Imprint of HarperCollins*Publishers*
10 East 53rd Street, New York, NY 10022.

Book created and produced by Parachute Publishing, L.L.C., in cooperation with Dualstar Publications, a division of Dualstar Entertainment Group, Inc., published by HarperEntertainment, an imprint of HarperCollins Publishers.

For information address HarperCollins Publishers Inc.,
10 East 53rd Street, New York, NY 10022.

ISBN 0-06-052053-1

HarperCollins®, **▲**®, and HarperEntertainment™ are trademarks of HarperCollins Publishers Inc.

First printing: November 2002

Printed in the United States of America

mary-kateandashley.com
America Online Keyword: mary-kateandashley

Visit HarperEntertainment on the World Wide Web at
www.harpercollins.com

CHAPTER ONE

"Roma!" Charli Hunter cried as she yanked open the long red drapes that covered the hotel room's French doors. "We're really in Rome!"

Charli's sister, Leila, leaped out of bed and joined her on the balcony. Below them lay the glorious rooftops of one of the most beautiful cities on earth. "Amazing," Leila breathed.

It sure is, Charli thought. She hadn't been able to see very much when they arrived late last night.

"Look at those cathedrals! Can you believe Rome is 2,700 years old?" Leila said. "There's big-time history here. Like, the Roman Empire...gladiators...Michelangelo..."

"And don't forget Versace," Charli joked.

She couldn't help it. Fashion was practically always on her mind. In fact, fabulous internships at the famous Hammond International were why the girls were here in Rome this summer.

Leila just laughed and ducked back into their bedroom to grab her 35mm camera. She was a serious photographer and always took pictures wherever they went. Quickly, she snapped a few shots of the amazing view.

1

"Do you think we'll actually get to work on a real fashion shoot this summer?" she asked her sister.

"Doubtful," Charli replied. "We're just interns, remember?" She sighed. "But isn't Rome the most romantic place on earth?"

"Probably," Leila said. "But hey, we're here to learn about the fashion industry. I'm not looking for a boyfriend. Even a cute Italian one."

"Mmm," Charli said. "Right. Me, too."

From the balcony, the two girls suddenly heard someone knocking hard on their bedroom door.

"You're late! It's nine o'clock!" a voice called.

"Oops! We must have messed up when we set our watches ahead on the plane," Leila said, dashing toward the bedroom.

Charli rushed after her sister and scrambled to get ready. But even as she turned on the water in the huge, marble bathroom, she couldn't help smiling.

This was going to be the most amazing summer, Charli decided. Just a *tiny* bit better than working at the mall back home in Los Angeles, California!

A few minutes later, she and Leila were dressed and set to go. Charli carefully tucked a small sketchpad into her bag. She wanted to be ready to draw her fashion ideas whenever the inspiration hit her.

The girls hurried into the hallway and ran smack into a group of four other kids their age—about fifteen years old.

"Ow! Oh, excuse me!" Charli cried.

She started to topple sideways, but one of the guys she'd slammed into caught her in his arms.

"*Scusi,*" he said, apologizing in Italian.

Charli gazed up into the boy's deep blue eyes. His longish black hair flopped forward a little, making him look as if he'd just rolled out of bed.

Wow. Is this the cutest guy I've seen in, like, ever? Charli wondered.

He smiled down at her, still holding her in his arms. "I am Paolo," he said softly.

"And I'm impressed," Charli blurted out. Then she corrected herself. "I mean, uh, I'm Charli."

Just then Jami Martin, a beautiful American woman in her thirties, strode toward them in the hallway. She was the coordinator of the internship program and their chaperone at the palazzo.

"Paolo, you can let Charli go now," Jami said.

"But why?" Paolo asked with a grin. The other interns laughed as Paolo took his arms away.

Yep, this is going to be an awesome summer, all right, Charli thought.

Jami smiled at all of them. "Welcome to Rome!" she said, spreading her arms wide. "And welcome to your summer jobs with Hammond International."

Just to make sure they were all up to speed, Jami gave them a quick recap of what Hammond International was all about.

Charli already knew everything by heart. Derek Hammond was a famous billionaire who ran an airline, a music company, a fashion company, several magazines, and tons more companies. He had offices in Rome, London, New York, and Tokyo.

This internship was just the beginning of what could be a fabulous string of exciting opportunities. Mr. Hammond was going to pick the best two interns from this summer and invite them to work in his New York offices next year!

It was so perfect. Charli had always dreamed of becoming a fashion designer someday. Now she was plunged right into the middle of the coolest fashion scene in the world!

And if I play my cards right, I could be spending next summer in New York! Charli couldn't help adding to herself.

"So that means we're all in competition with one another, right?" one of the other girls asked Jami.

Charli turned around. The girl looked athletic. She had short blond hair and was wearing slim khaki pants with a white sleeveless top.

"Well, yes," Jami said, nodding. "But I don't want you to put too much energy into competing."

"But Mr. Hammond's only going to pick two of us," the girl said. "That means four people are going to lose. Right?"

Charli's back stiffened at the hostile vibe. *Could*

this girl be any more competitive? she wondered.

Jami didn't seem to like the blond girl's attitude, either. "Just do your best," Jami said. "Don't expect yourselves to be perfect." She smiled at the group. "Let's introduce ourselves before we head over to the office. Obviously, Charli and Paolo have already met. Paolo is from right here in Rome. Let's start with Paolo's roommate. How about it, Nobu?"

A cute, shy Japanese guy with great dimples smiled and almost bowed. "Hi," he said to everyone. "I'm Nobu, from Tokyo."

Jami nodded and turned to the other two girls, who were rooming together across the hall from Charli and Leila.

"I'm Dari," a pretty girl with thick black hair spoke up. "From Venice."

Beside her, the blond girl didn't bother to smile. "Heidi," she said curtly. "Munich, Germany."

"My sister, Charli, and I are from L.A.," Leila said.

"Okay, great," Jami said. "Now just one more thing before we go. Derek Hammond wants you all to enjoy your jobs this summer, but he does have one firm rule. No dating among the interns. Got that?"

No way! Charli thought, glancing at Paolo. *What fun is that?* She blushed when she saw Paolo look back at her.

Jami clapped her hands. "Okay, interns, we're late already," she said. "Let's run!"

The six of them followed Jami down the palazzo steps and out into the sunny Roman streets. They hurried on the narrow sidewalks through crowds of people walking toward the center of Rome. Vespas and other motorbikes whizzed by.

Moments later, they turned a corner and came upon one of the most beautiful spots in Rome.

"There they are," Paolo announced, with a sweep of his arm. "Piazza di Spagna—the Spanish Steps, you Americans say."

Charli and the others stopped dead in their tracks and gazed upward. The Spanish Steps were a wide, terraced staircase set into the side of one of Rome's famous seven hills. At the top of the steps was a church and another small street lined with hotels and shops.

"Our offices are up there," Jami said. "Let's go!"

"We're in Rome, but we're on *Spanish* steps," Charli said as they climbed to the top. "Weird, huh?"

"Is that what you Americans call a joke?" Paolo asked.

"No," Heidi said with a smirk. "Jokes are funny."

Ouch! Charli thought, cringing.

"What's *her* problem?" Leila whispered.

"I don't know," Charli whispered back. "But I'll tell you one thing. If we want to get invited to New York next summer, we'll have to get past *her* first!"

CHAPTER TWO

When they finally reached the top of the killer Spanish Steps, Charli turned around and gasped. "You can see all of Rome from here!" she said to Leila.

For a moment, the two of them stopped to take in the view of St. Peter's Basilica and the Vatican. Then they ran to catch up with Jami. She had led the group down a small, narrow street toward a café near the Hammond International offices.

"We're having an introductory breakfast first," Jami explained. "Signor Tortoni has set up it for us."

"*Benvenuto*," a well-dressed man greeted them, gesturing to the seats. "Welcome."

"*Grazie*," Charli replied, pleased to be using the little Italian she had learned so far. "Isn't this great service?" she whispered to Leila. "I love Italian waiters!"

Leila nodded. "And I am *so* thirsty. Could I please get an orange juice?" she asked the waiter.

"Iced tea for me," Nobu said, sitting down.

"Do you have bagels by any chance?" Charli asked.

Heidi cleared her throat. "*Buongiorno*, Signor Tortoni," she said, smirking at the others.

Jami shifted uncomfortably on her feet. "Um,

interns, may I introduce Signor Enrico Tortoni—the head of our office here in Rome. You'll be working directly for him this summer."

He's not our waiter? Charli felt herself blush. *Major mistake. And on my first day, too!*

Heidi barely tried to hide her gloating smile. "It's going to be *so* easy to get to New York next year," she muttered under her breath.

"I'm really sorry, Mr. Tortoni," Charli said quickly. "I thought...I mean..."

"No offense taken, Charli," Mr. Tortoni said.

"You know her name?" Leila blurted out.

Mr. Tortoni nodded. "I know *all* your names, Signorina Leila," he said. "You will be working for me, so it's good that I know, no?"

"I thought we were working for Derek Hammond," Dari said.

"Well, technically, you are," Jami explained. "But Mr. Hammond is a very busy man."

"Sorry to disappoint you." Mr. Tortoni shrugged. "Mr. Hammond is in New York one day, Paris the next. Me, I am always here. And *you,*" he added with a pause, "you are all forty-seven minutes late."

Was he serious? Charli wondered. They'd only been in Rome for about eight hours. She and Leila had gotten practically no sleep.

"But, Mr. Tortoni—" Jami began to explain.

A smile turned up at the corners of his mouth.

"Jami, I'm just joking. Now please, everyone, enjoy your breakfast. I'll see all of you in the office." He started to walk away, but then turned back with a stern expression on his face. "In exactly fifteen minutes," he said.

Charli froze. Was that another joke? If so, it definitely didn't meet Heidi's test for funny.

"Just kidding," Mr. Tortoni said, smiling. "Enjoy your meal. But when you arrive at work today, I want all of you to give me your best. As you know, we picked you from hundreds of applicants. I expect a very high level of performance. But right now I have a meeting. *Arrivederci.*"

When Mr. Tortoni had left, Charli glanced around the table at the other interns. Everyone looked confused, just like she felt. Except for Heidi. The expression on her face said: "If Tortoni wants to play tough, that's fine with me. Bring it on!"

Okay, Charli thought. *If Heidi wants to play tough, I can bring it on, too!*

After a delicious Italian breakfast of cappuccino and *cornetti*, which was the Italian word for croissants, they all headed to Hammond International next door. Jami handed out their assignments.

"Dari and Nobu will do some photocopying," Jami said. "Charli and Paolo, you two will deliver packages today."

"*Brava!*" Paolo cried.

"Can you ride a Vespa, Charli?" Jami asked.

"Yes!" Charli answered quickly. "I mean, no—but I'm ready to learn."

"Good," Jami said. "Paolo will teach you. Your helmets and packages are by the back door."

Pinch me! Charli told herself. Was this for real? Could her life possibly get any better?

"Come with me," Paolo said, shooting her a huge smile.

In a heartbeat, Charli thought. "I love this job!" she whispered to Leila on her way out.

As she and Paolo left, Charli heard Jami tell Leila that she would be teamed up with Heidi to deliver the mail inside the office.

Poor Leila, Charli thought. *She's stuck with the Ice Queen, and I'll be riding a Vespa with the cutest guy in Rome!*

When they were outside with their helmets on, Paolo hopped on to a small red motorbike. "Climb on," he told Charli. "The best way to learn is to ride behind me. Hold on tight, okay?"

Whatever you say! Charli thought happily as she wrapped her arms around his waist.

Paolo took off, zooming down the narrow, hilly streets and darting in and out of traffic.

"Don't lean too much with the bike," he instructed her. "Just sit normally, and let your body go where the bike wants you to go."

"Okay." Charli nodded.

Then Paolo showed her how the gas and brakes worked. She also learned how to start slowly so the bike wouldn't take off with a jerk.

"Got it?" he asked.

"I think so," Charli said.

"Okay. Now I will take you somewhere," Paolo said as he zoomed toward the center of the city.

"Where are we going?" Charli asked. If her sense of direction was right, the office was pretty far behind them by now. "What about the packages?"

"Don't worry about packages," Paola said. "First I must show you my Roma!"

"No way," Charli protested. "We're supposed to be making a delivery. We have a *job* to do, remember?"

"But we *are* doing a job," Paolo said with a laugh. "I am delivering *you* to the most beautiful city in the world!"

Charli started to argue—sort of. But she was having too much fun to put up a fight.

What am I doing? she wondered. *It's my very first day at work, and I'm just skipping out on the job.*

That definitely wasn't like her. At all.

And she usually didn't go for guys who couldn't take anything seriously, either. But there was something different about Paolo....

He doesn't really *seem like someone who would blow off responsibilities,* she thought.

She wrapped her arms tighter around his waist as he weaved in and out on the streets.

"So you like Roma?" Paolo called over the noise.

"It's amazing!" Charli answered truthfully. She couldn't help watching everything speeding by—the buildings, the churches, the cafés, the people. "Oh wow, is that the Colosseum?"

"Yes," Paolo said. "It was built two thousand years ago. That is where men and some women did battle to the death."

"I saw *Gladiator* twice," Charli shouted.

"*Mamma mia!* I am talking about *real* history!" Paolo cried.

"So you didn't see *Gladiator*?" Charli asked.

"Well, maybe," Paolo admitted. "Four times."

Charli laughed as he zoomed past the Colosseum without stopping. A few minutes later, he returned to the Hammond offices, and Charli climbed off.

"Okay," he said. "You're ready to drive. It's easy."

It took a few minutes of practice, but Charli caught on pretty quickly. Then she and Paolo strapped the packages onto their two bikes and zoomed off again.

"Via Benedetta," Charli called, hoping he could hear her. "That's where we're supposed to go. Do you know where it is?"

Paolo didn't answer. He led the way, weaving in and out of traffic again, past ancient buildings and beautiful piazzas with huge stone carved fountains.

Twenty minutes later, he finally pulled over.

"Is this it?" Charli asked, glancing around.

Paolo took out a slip of paper with the address on it and stared.

Uh-oh, Charli thought. *He definitely looks lost.*

"Do you have any idea where we're going?" she asked him.

With a big grin, Paolo shook his head no.

"Well, do you know where we are *now*?" she asked.

Again, he shook his head no.

"I don't believe this," Charli said. "You've lived here your whole life. *I* was following *you*!"

"You can live in Roma one hundred years and not know all of these crazy streets," Paolo said.

Charli eyed him sideways. Was he kidding? Why had he even bothered to apply for this job if he didn't want to do it well?

Her heart began to pound a little. Would they get in trouble with Mr. Tortoni?

Charli took a deep breath. "Okay, stay calm," she said, mostly to herself. She reached into the small storage compartment on her Vespa. "We're cool—we have a map."

"A map?" Paolo grabbed it and tossed it into a nearby trash can. "You are so American!"

"What's wrong with that?" Charli asked, feeling annoyed.

"Nothing," Paolo said. "But you Americans are always in a hurry. Italians, we like to take our time. What's the rush?"

"Paolo, we've been gone from the office nearly two hours! Just to deliver two packages!" Charli frowned. "This is *not* the kind of impression I want to make on my first day."

Paolo saw the worried look on her face and sighed. "Okay, okay," he said. He pulled a cell phone out of his pocket, dialed a number, and said something in Italian to the person on the other line. "Problem solved," he announced.

"It is?" Charli asked. "Did you get directions?"

"Wait and see," Paolo said mysteriously.

"Wait and see?" Charli asked. "What does that mean?"

Paolo shrugged.

This is getting ridiculous, Charli thought. "Listen, I am so close to getting in your face—" she began.

"I have no problem with our faces being close," Paolo teased, moving a little closer to her.

Now what am I going to do? Charli wondered. He was so cute. And the playful look in his eyes said: I don't take anything seriously—except flirting!

Just then a vintage black Vespa zipped into the piazza and skidded to a stop next to them. The rider jumped off, grabbed the packages from their bikes, and dropped them into a bin on the back of his.

"Hey!" Charli cried. "Stop him! He took our packages!"

"I know," Paolo said, grinning. "I called him. My friend Vittorio has delivered pizzas to every address in Rome. Now he will deliver our packages for us. And we can spend time together, not worrying. Yes?"

"*Bella!*" Vittorio called, glancing at Charli as he zoomed away.

"What did he say?" Charli asked.

"He said you were beautiful," Paolo replied. "And I agree. So can we forget about the internship for a little while?"

Oh no, Charli thought. *What am I getting myself into? I'll never get picked to go to New York!*

But the packages *were* on their way to being delivered—right? And she wanted to have *some* fun this summer.

"Well, okay," Charli said finally. "But just for an hour."

"What's an hour?" Paolo said. "This is Roma!"

"Italian boys," Charli muttered, shaking her head.

Paolo grinned. "I take that as a compliment," he said.

CHAPTER THREE

"You've got the wrong pile of mail," Heidi pointed out loudly to Leila.

Leila pushed her long, wavy blond hair out of her eyes and glanced around the large, open-design Hammond International offices. Everyone was staring up at them from their desks, trying to see what the problem was.

Why don't you just relax? Leila wanted to tell her.

But with everyone watching, she wasn't going to say anything. Instead, she bit her tongue and continued pushing the mail cart down the aisle. There were big, open cubicles along each side.

Charli was right, she thought. *Heidi is going to be a major pain this summer.*

"This stack goes to the director of music promotions," Leila said quietly. "I don't have the wrong pile."

"Whatever." Heidi shrugged. "Go ahead, if you think you know what you're doing. But if anyone gets the wrong mail, it's not my fault." Her voice grew louder and louder, so everyone could hear.

What is *your problem?* Leila thought.

That was a dumb question. Heidi was really easy to read, like a book with just one sentence: "Make all the other interns look bad so I'll get the job in New York next summer."

Leila tried to ignore her partner and kept working. *This place is totally awesome,* she thought. Even handing out mail was kind of fun. Most of the people at Hammond were young, and they all looked so...so Italian! They were dressed in the hippest, coolest clothes and had tons of style.

A young woman in a cubicle behind them cleared her throat. "Excuse me," she called. "This isn't for me." She waved a large manila envelope.

Leila heard Heidi snicker.

"Wrong name," the woman said, flipping her tiny black glasses up onto her head.

"Oh." Leila walked back to the woman's cubicle and took the envelope. "Sorry, but I didn't give you that. She did."

"Hey, it's no big deal," the woman said. "Don't push the blame onto someone else. Just get it right next time."

But I didn't do it! Leila wanted to say.

"I told you to be careful," Heidi said in a really phony voice, as if she were trying to help Leila out.

Leila couldn't believe it. Heidi really *was* trying to make her look bad on purpose!

"Um, can I have a word with you, please?" Leila motioned the blond girl toward a quiet hallway.

Heidi shrugged and followed her.

"Look, I know what's going on here," Leila said. "We *all* want to do well this summer. But you aren't going to get that spot in New York next year by trying to make me look stupid. You've got to earn it on your own."

"I have no idea what you're talking about," Heidi said. Then she spun around and walked away.

Leila sighed. All the other interns were so nice. Why did Heidi have to be such a creep?

When Leila got back to the mail cart, Heidi was nowhere in sight. Great. Now she'd left her with all the rest of the work!

But maybe it was better that way, Leila decided. A lot less hassle.

She pushed the cart through the offices, leaving a pile of mail on each desk.

The last batch was a whole bin of mail addressed to Mr. Tortoni. The sign on his office door said PRIVATE but Leila wanted to make absolutely sure he got his mail. She slipped into Mr. Tortoni's office and set the bin on a clean spot on his desk.

Nice, she thought, looking around. There were four big corkboards on one wall—one for each division of Hammond. The fashion board was totally cool. It was covered with sketches of all the new clothes they were working on for next spring.

Leila's eye caught a glimpse of a sketch on Mr. Tortoni's desk. It was a wedding dress—with pants!

She leaned in to get a closer look.

"Signorina Hunter! What are you doing in my office?" Mr. Tortoni said from the doorway.

Leila jumped and whirled around. "Oh! Sorry, I was just bringing in your mail." She gestured toward the bin on his desk.

Mr. Tortoni rushed to his desk and started gathering up papers. "I don't appreciate you snooping around in my office when I'm not here, Leila," he said coldly.

"But I *wasn't* snooping," Leila protested. "Honest. I just—"

"Never mind." Mr. Tortoni was still grabbing papers off his desk and stuffing them into a drawer. "I'll let it go this time," he said. "In fact, I'll give you a chance to prove you have a good head on your shoulders." Mr. Tortoni jotted down an address on a slip of paper. "Go to this shop and pick up a hat for Mr. Hammond's private pilot."

"A pilot's hat?" Leila said.

"Yes," Mr. Tortoni said. "You can handle that, I hope?"

"Of course," Leila said. She looked at the address. "Is this the hat shop I saw on the way here? At the bottom of the Spanish Steps?"

"No," Mr. Tortoni said. "I'm afraid not. This one is far away from here."

"Well, okay, Mr. Tortoni," Leila said. "That's not

a problem at all. I'll be back here as soon as I can."

"Take your time," he said, waving.

That's weird, Leila thought. It almost sounded like he was trying to get rid of her!

But why? Because he thought she was snooping through his stuff?

Mr. Tortoni stared at her, waiting for her to leave, so Leila hurried out.

She checked the big map that was posted on the wall in the employees lounge. The hat shop was within walking distance—but it was a long walk.

Who cares? Leila thought. *It's a beautiful day—and I'm in Rome!*

She had to go down all 137 Spanish Steps on her way. They were crowded by now, too. It wasn't easy making her way through the clusters of tourists taking pictures, and the gazillion teenagers who were just hanging out.

Wow, Leila thought. *This must be the social center of Rome!* It seemed as if the steps were the place where everyone came just to relax and take in the street life.

Finally she found the hat store. The owner didn't speak English, but Leila gestured and he smiled and they worked it out.

An hour later, she huffed her way back up the Spanish Steps and into the Hammond offices with the hatbox in hand.

"Leila! Mr. Tortoni wants you in his office!" Jami said.

"Sure, what's up?" Leila asked.

"I don't know," Jami said, "but he's called everyone in, including Charli and Paolo. And he looks very unhappy."

Leila swallowed hard. All the other interns were standing stiffly in Mr. Tortoni's office by the time Leila got there.

"Glad you could join us, Signorina Hunter," he said coolly. "Did you bring the hat?"

"No problem." Leila handed it to him.

Mr. Tortoni peeked inside the box, then set it on his desk. "I must say, I am very disappointed in you interns," he said. "Dari and Nobu, you made two hundred forty copies of the wrong document."

Nobu opened his mouth to protest, but Mr. Tortoni held up his hand for silence.

How did that happen? Leila asked herself. And why did she have a funny feeling Heidi had something to do with it?

"Would you like *me* to copy the document correctly?" Heidi offered in a super-sweet voice.

Mr. Tortoni shook his head. "Never mind, thank you, Heidi," he said. "Paolo and Charli, you were supposed to be delivering fabric. Instead, our customers got pepperoni pizzas. And Leila..."

"Is there a problem with the hat?" she asked.

21

Mr. Tortoni reached inside the box—and pulled out a tall white chef's hat!

"Does this look like a pilot's cap to you?" he snapped. "Mr. Hammond's pilot would look ridiculous in this thing!"

Huh? Leila thought. She was *sure* the guy in the hat shop had understood! "I'm sorry, sir," she said quickly. "There's no excuse."

"No, there isn't," Mr. Tortoni said. He paced for a moment with his hands behind his back and a tight look on his face. "Interns, I dislike saying this, but so far, Heidi is the only person I feel I can count on. Everyone else is on probation."

"Probation?" Jami broke in. "Oh, Mr. Tortoni, please—it's their first day. I'm sure—"

Mr. Tortoni sighed. "Fine. Preliminary probation."

"Preliminary probation?" Charli asked. "What's that?"

Mr. Tortoni frowned. "It means that next time..." He stopped. "Let's just say there better not *be* a next time—or your summer job will be over before it's begun!"

CHAPTER FOUR

"Can you believe we almost got fired on our first day?" Charli said as she, Leila, and the other interns walked toward the Piazza Navona after work.

"Our parents would freak if we got sent home," Leila said. "And besides, this internship is really important to me. I want to learn all I can about fashion photography."

"Hey, just concentrate on doing things right and you'll be fine," Heidi advised.

"Do things right? Easy for you to say," Nobu said. "You lucked out with interoffice mail."

"Mail is easier than *copying*?" Heidi said in a mocking tone. "Please. A monkey could have done your job!"

"Stop it!" Leila said. "We're a team, remember?"

"That's right," Paolo said. "And this is your first day in Rome. Can we—how you say?—chill and have some fun?"

"Fun is what got me in trouble," Charli told him under her breath.

Paolo moved closer to her and started to slip his arm around Charli's waist. But she moved away.

"No dating among the interns, remember?" she

said in a low voice so that Jami wouldn't hear her.

That rule is the worst, she thought. *But maybe I should stick to it—for my own good!*

Then Paolo shot her a smile and she almost melted. There was something about him...something totally honest and real. It was as if he had some kind of secret that made him special. Charli just didn't know what it was.

Jami was about ten steps ahead of the group, leading the way. A moment later, she turned into a narrow passageway between two buildings. And there it was: one of the most popular and beautiful piazzas in Rome.

Charli stared at the piazza—a huge, enclosed square surrounded by two- and three-story buildings. Bustling cafés were located on the ground floors. In the center of the square was a huge, magnificent fountain. Its tall, carved stone figures of buff Roman gods with water pouring from their mouths were totally awesome.

"Oh, look! Street artists! I want to have my portrait drawn," Dari declared.

"This is an incredible place to take pictures," Leila said. She pulled out her camera and began snapping away.

"How about a photo of the internship director in front of the fountain?" Jami called.

"Sure." Leila stepped back and checked the scene.

"Just move a bit to your right. It's a more intriguing background."

"You're really serious about photography, aren't you?" Jami asked.

"Definitely," Leila said. "Capturing an image? Creating a lasting memory? Totally cool."

"Sounds like you have some real goals," Jami said.

"I do," Leila said. "If things go well this summer, maybe someday I'll work for you."

Jami smiled. "Did you know that Fillitti, the famous fashion photographer, will be shooting our new spring line next week?" she said.

"Fillitti? You're kidding!" Leila's mouth dropped open. "It would be so awesome to watch him work!"

"Do your job well, and I'll see if I can get you invited to the photo session," Jami said with a wink.

"But first you have to survive being on probation," Heidi reminded her.

Charli frowned. That girl really knew how to ruin a good conversation—and fast!

Jami didn't seem to have heard Heidi's mean comment. "Okay, interns, have fun," their chaperone called to the group. "Let's meet back here, at the base of the fountain, in two hours."

Charli glanced at Paolo, wondering what he wanted to do. He nodded to her, and together they strolled around to the far end of the fountain, away from the group.

"Let the others get their portraits drawn," he said quietly. "Come with me."

Charli followed him. She didn't want her portrait done, anyway. It would be a lot more fun to just wander with Paolo and watch all the people.

When they were farther away, he gently took her hand.

She definitely didn't want to let go—but she didn't want to get into any more trouble for dating an intern, either.

"Oh, look!" she said, pulling her hand away and pretending she needed it to point at a mime standing near the fountain.

Paolo laughed. "You American girls are so tight up," he teased her.

"You mean uptight," Charli corrected him.

"*Si*. Uptight."

So what if I am? Charli thought. She put a hand on her hip. "Tell me, how do you know so many American girls, anyway?"

"Uh-oh. I'm in trouble now, no?" Paolo said.

"Definitely," Charli told him, but she smiled to let him know she was only kidding.

"Well, I meet many tourists," Paolo said. He sat down on the edge of the fountain and motioned for Charli to sit beside him.

"Now you're getting in even more trouble," Charli teased as she sat down. "Much more."

"No, no, I don't mean I'm flirting with them," Paolo explained. "I meet them at work."

"At work? Let me guess," Charli said. "You drive a tour bus. No, that wouldn't work with your—what do we Americans say?—*zero sense of direction.*"

To her surprise, Paolo didn't answer.

That was a joke, Paolo, Charli told him silently. *Laugh!*

But he had a faraway look in his eyes right then, as if he was thinking about something really important. "Someday I show you," he said quietly.

Hmm, Charli thought. He obviously *did* have a secret. But what was it?

"Okay, maybe you work at the airport," Charli said, trying to tease him out of his quiet mood. "You'd meet a lot of American girls there. But no, you'd have to be on time for a job like that. So maybe—"

Suddenly Paolo leaned forward and placed one finger on her lips. "Relax," he said. "You're in Italy—be Italian! Be—what do you say?—mellow. Hang loosely. Chill. Have fun." He took her hand again.

For half a second, Charli thought of pulling it away. What if Jami came by and saw them?

But she couldn't turn away. Not now. Paolo was too nice, too cute, and this was way too much fun.

CHAPTER FIVE

"You're stuck delivering mail with Heidi *again*?" Charli said to her sister the next morning.

"I can deal with it." Leila sighed. "I mean, we're interns, right? What's your assignment?"

"Worse," Charli said. "Tortoni has me making coffee. But I've never seen a coffee machine like this before. It's huge!"

"Not coffee," Paolo said, popping his head into the employee's lounge. "Espresso. Very different."

"Whatever," Charli said.

"At least you're working with Paolo again," Leila whispered. "That's good, right?"

Charli nodded. "Very good."

"I'm off to get the *cornetti*," Paolo said.

"Hey, wait," Charli said. "I thought you were going to show me how to work the espresso machine."

"I leave instructions. In English. Very simple. Few steps," Paolo said. "*Ciao*."

Charli groaned and went to struggle with the coffee machine.

Leila gathered up the mail and put it on a cart. *Where's Heidi?* she wondered, looking around. Then she saw her in Mr. Tortoni's office.

Probably trying to butter him up, Leila thought.

She pushed the mail cart toward the boss's office and stepped inside.

"So how did Mr. Hammond get into so many businesses?" Heidi was asking. "Fashion, airlines, music...they're all so different."

"Not really," Leila spoke up. "The magazine promotes the fashion and recording artists. The artists wear the fashions. And you push the magazines and music on the airlines, right, Mr. Tortoni?"

"Yes," he said. "It's called vertical integration—a very smart business plan. And you, Signorina Hunter, are a very smart young lady."

Leila smiled uneasily. *If that was a compliment,* she thought, *then why is he frowning?*

"Do you like music, Leila?" Mr. Tortoni asked.

Leila nodded. "Sure."

"I see. Well, this is a hot new artist we just recorded at our London studios." He handed her a CD. "I want you girls to deliver this to Signor Piranesi. He is my inside source at Roma's top radio station. He'll play it on the air today."

"Thank you!" Leila said eagerly. "We'll take care of it right away." This was an important errand—a real chance to prove herself! After the snooping incident yesterday, she'd been afraid Mr. Tortoni might never give her a chance again.

"And anytime you want to talk, Leila, my door is

29

always open," Mr. Tortoni added. "Remember that."

"Thanks," Leila said. She glanced over at Heidi. The girl did *not* look happy.

It seemed as if Mr. Tortoni wanted them to leave, so Leila and Heidi took the CD and headed out of the building. Halfway to the door, Leila realized they didn't have the address of the radio station.

"Oops, we need the address. Wait here. I'll go get it," Leila said. On the way back to Mr. Tortoni's office, she popped her head into the coffee room. "How's it going?" she asked Charli.

"Don't ask," Charli moaned. "I can't even figure out where the coffee goes!"

"You want some help?" Leila offered.

"No time," Charli said. "I'm just going to make instant coffee."

"Okay," Leila said, dashing off to Mr. Tortoni's office. When she got there, he was standing with his back to the door, talking on the phone.

"No, I don't have them yet," he was saying. "But I have a plan to get them. It may take me another day or two."

Leila waited, not wanting to interrupt.

"Yes," Mr. Tortoni went on. "All the designs. You'll have them before the shoot."

What's that about? Leila wondered. Jami had mentioned the big fashion shoot next week. All the new spring fashions were being finished right now.

But why would he give someone the Hammond designs *before* the shoot?

Just then Mr. Tortoni turned and caught Leila watching him. "I can't speak right now," he said abruptly into the phone. "I'll call you later." Mr. Tortoni slammed down the phone and glared at Leila. "Signorina Hunter, I know I said my door is always open, but I didn't mean for you to stand there, listening to my conversations."

"I came back for the address," Leila said weakly. "You, um, forgot to give it to me."

"*You* forgot to ask for it," Mr. Tortoni corrected her. He scrawled an address on a slip of paper and handed it to her. "Remember, you are on probation," he said. "Don't make a mistake this time."

"I won't," Leila promised, and hurried out.

She thought about what she'd just overheard. It sounded kind of strange. Or was she just being extra sensitive with Tortoni because he was on her case?

He was definitely acting guilty, she thought.

But guilty of what?

She decided to forget the whole thing—at least for now. She and Heidi had a job to do, and she did not want to mess up this time.

It only took the girls twenty minutes to find the radio station. Leila was beginning to feel as though she already knew her way around the city.

"I wonder who's on that CD?" Heidi said, staring

at the disc in Leila's hands. She tapped her CD player, which was hooked onto her jeans. "Let's listen to it first."

"No thanks," Leila said. "I don't want to get into any more trouble, okay?"

Heidi shrugged. "Hey, that's your problem, not mine," she said. "Let's just listen to one song." She reached for the CD and grabbed hold of one side.

"No way!" Leila said, jerking her hand back.

Heidi gave a second pull on the CD, and the jewel case came open. The CD fell out and rolled into the street.

"Oh, no!" Leila cried. She started to dash out into the street to grab the disc. But a guy on a Vespa was zooming right toward them. She had to jump back out of the way.

Leila watched the Vespa in horror. In two seconds the driver was going to ride over the CD. Tortoni would never forgive her.

I'm dead! she thought, covering her eyes.

But somehow, miraculously, the CD didn't break.

"I can't believe it," Leila gasped. "It's a miracle."

"Those things are pretty tough," Heidi said. She sounded sort of disappointed.

Leila narrowed her eyes. *Did Heidi do that on purpose, so the CD would get trashed and I'd be fired?* she wondered.

Leila stooped down to pick up the disc before

anything else could happen—just as a dog ran up and scooped it into his mouth like a Frisbee.

"Hey! Wait!" Leila yelled as the dog ran off with the CD. The dog disappeared down an alley.

"Oh, well," Heidi said. "Bad luck, I guess."

Bad luck? Leila stared at her. It was a nightmare! Then her heart sunk all the way to her knees. "What are we going to tell Tortoni?" she asked.

"The truth," Heidi said, shrugging. "What else?" She began to trudge back toward the Hammond offices.

Leila sighed and followed her. Heidi was right. The two of them would have to come clean.

Then Leila felt a tiny spring of hope. Maybe if Heidi took responsibility, too, Tortoni wouldn't be so mad.

She'd just have to hope for another miracle.

"That was the worst coffee I've ever tasted in my life!" Leila heard Mr. Tortoni shouting as she and Heidi reached his office.

Their boss paced up and down, fuming. The other interns were lined up along the wall, looking as if they were ready to meet their doom.

Uh-oh, Leila thought. *Major trouble. Again.*

Now was definitely not a good time to tell Mr. Tortoni what had happened to the CD.

He whirled around and spotted Leila and Heidi.

"The radio station called," he said, glaring at them. "They want to know where the CD is."

"We lost it, I'm afraid, Signor Tortoni," Heidi admitted.

"Lost it? But how is that possible?" Mr. Tortoni exploded. "I gave you a responsibility and you were irresponsible!" He began to rant in a flood of Italian.

"I am so sorry, sir," Leila said. "But it wasn't my fault."

"I hear that too often from my American interns." He glared over his shoulder at Charli, then turned back again. "Do you have anything to add, Heidi?"

Come on, Heidi, Leila thought. *The truth.* She held her breath.

"It was an accident, Signor Tortoni," Heidi said.

Leila closed her eyes in relief.

"But it was completely preventable," Heidi went on. "I warned Leila not to open that CD."

Are you kidding me? Leila stared daggers at Heidi. But there was nothing she could say. Tortoni probably wouldn't believe her, anyway.

"We hired you to help us, not disappoint us," Mr. Tortoni went on. "So, in the interest of Hammond International, you are fired, Signorina Leila."

"Fired?" Leila was stunned.

"That is correct," Mr. Tortoni said. "In fact, you and your sister are *both* terminated. And you're going home—tonight."

34

CHAPTER SIX

"How can we possibly go home just forty-eight hours after we got to Italy?" Charli moaned.

The girls were sadly pulling their suitcases behind them as they followed Jami toward a small city square. They had to check in at the airport soon. But first Jami had insisted that they stop for a last look at one of Rome's most famous spots.

"The thing is," Leila whispered to her sister, "I have a feeling Tortoni was *trying* to get rid of me. I mean, *us*. I think he might be up to something."

"Because of that phone call you overheard?" Charli asked. Leila had told Charli all about it back at the palazzo.

"Yes. And those papers on his desk that he was trying to hide," Leila said. "And the fact that he fired you for making bad coffee. I mean, that's just too weird. I don't care *how* serious Italians are about their coffee."

"Espresso." Charli sighed. "But what did Tortoni say on the phone, anyway?"

"I can't remember his exact words, but it was something about trying to get the designs—all of them—in a few days," Leila said, still keeping her voice low. "And when he saw me he said 'I can't talk now,' and hung up."

"But he already *has* the designs," Charli said, puzzled. "Why would he be trying to *get* them?"

Leila sighed. "That's the strange part."

"Maybe we should tell Jami," Charli whispered.

Leila shook her head. "We can't prove anything," she said. "It would just sound like we were mad for getting fired."

Just then Jami peeked around a corner and turned to the girls with a big smile on her face.

"Here it is!" she announced. "Trevi Fountain. Every tourist on the planet comes here when they visit this city."

Charli took in the gorgeous fountain in front of them. It sprang from the side of a wall at the base of a building. Water flowed over carvings of rocks, flowers, horses, and Roman gods.

"I really hate to leave," she said. "Jami, isn't there any chance...?" Her voiced trailed off.

Jami looked sympathetic. "I'm sorry, girls," she said. "I don't think it was fair of Mr. Tortoni to fire you, either. I've left three messages for Derek Hammond. But who knows where he is right now?"

Charli watched as a crowd of tourists walked up to the fountain and tossed in some coins. Leila snapped a few last pictures.

"Go on," Jami said, "Throw in a couple of coins

yourselves. You know what they say: Throw a coin in the Trevi Fountain, and you'll be sure to return to Rome."

Charli shook her head. "No thanks," she said glumly. "After this whole disaster, I don't think we'll be rushing back here anytime soon."

"I'm so embarrassed," Leila added. "I know I messed up with the hat and the CD, but it's totally humiliating to be sent home. And I was planning to learn so much about fashion...."

"You're being too hard on yourselves," Jami said. "I'm afraid Mr. Tortoni has been a little sensitive these past few months. I think he overreacted. You didn't deserve to be fired."

Sensitive? Charli and Leila exchanged glances. Was that another way of saying that Mr. Tortoni was acting fishy—and up to no good?

But there was no way for them to prove it. And no point in even trying. What for? They were going home.

"I don't want to be sent home!" Leila blurted out. "This was supposed to be the experience of a lifetime."

"I know," Charli agreed. A lump formed in her throat. "I thought I was going to see real fashion designing up close."

"I was going to watch Fillitti on a photo shoot!" Leila moaned.

And I was going to get to know Paolo better,
Charli added silently. They'd hardly even had a
chance to say good-bye.

All at once, Charli felt as if she was going to start
crying. Then she looked over at her sister. Tears were
beginning to form in Leila's eyes, too.

They were both about to lose it.

"Hey, cheer up," Charli said, trying to make a
joke. "Don't forget, we'll be going back to the mall
at home. And they do have a fountain there—not
quite as nice as this one, though."

Leila laughed a small laugh. Then she said, "You
know what? I'm just sorry we never even got to
meet Derek Hammond."

"And what would you do if you met him?" a
man's voice boomed.

Startled, Charli jumped, and Leila gasped. A
good-looking, well-dressed man had suddenly
stepped out of the crowd behind them.

"Mr. Hammond!" Jami cried, rushing forward.
"I was trying to reach you!"

"And you succeeded," he added, smiling warmly
at Jami. Their eyes lingered on each other for a few
seconds.

Whoa, Charli thought, feeling the chemistry
between the two.

Mr. Hammond cleared his throat and took a step
back. "I was in Florence, so I took the train down. I

understand Charli and Leila have a problem?"

"We messed up, Mr. Hammond," Leila said quickly. "We're so sorry."

"But we'd really like another chance," Charli added.

Hammond tilted his head and frowned. "Enrico Tortoni has been with Hammond International since the beginning," he said. "I trust him like a brother. And I don't like to overrule his decisions."

"Oh," Charli said. "I see."

Then a little smile crept into the corners of his mouth. "But nothing is final until I say it is," he added.

"Does that mean we can stay?" Leila asked, her eyes lighting up.

Mr. Hammond didn't answer. Instead, he reached into his pocket and handed each girl a coin. "Make a wish," he said.

Charli closed her eyes and stood with her back to the fountain, the way she'd seen the other people do. *I don't want to leave Rome,* she thought. *Please, please, please, let us stay!*

She tossed the coin over her shoulder and hoped with all her heart that the Trevi Fountain could work its magic.

CHAPTER SEVEN

"Your bags are packed, I see," Mr. Hammond said after Leila and Charli had made their wishes. "Good."

What's so good about that? Leila thought.

"My helicopter is on the tarmac," Mr. Hammond went on. "It's a thirty-minute ride to my villa by the sea. I'd like you two interns and Ms. Martin to join me for a few days of fun and sun."

"No way!" Leila gasped.

"Way," Derek Hammond said with a grin.

Charli grinned. "I guess our wishes are coming true already."

An hour later, the girls were lounging by Mr. Hammond's pool with Jami.

"Is this amazing or what?" Leila said. She held up her camera, aimed it over her shoulder, and pushed the button with her eyes closed.

"What are you doing?" Charli asked, glancing up from her sketching.

Leila shrugged. "There are so many spectacular shots here," she said. "I'm just proving that you can practically click away with your eyes closed, and the pictures will come out well."

"I wish I could say the same for my drawings," Charli said. She looked down at the sketchpad on her lap and frowned. "They aren't coming out that great, even with my eyes *open*!"

Jami leaned over from her lounge chair to look.

"It's just doodling," Charli said.

"It's way more than that," Leila spoke up.

Jami lifted her sunglasses and looked at the sketches again. "Leila's right, Charli. I've been in the fashion business ten years and those sketches are *way* beyond doodling. You're really talented! May I show these to Mr. Hammond?" she asked.

"Oh no, please! I mean, I don't think I'm ready for that," Charli insisted.

"Okay. It's your call," Jami said, sounding disappointed. "But I think you may have real potential."

"Thanks." Charli stood up from her lounge chair to look at the ocean. "You know, unemployment is not such a terrible thing," she said to her sister.

"Um, I don't know about that," Leila said. "This is a pretty sweet setup, but I want my job back."

"Oh, I want my job back, too," Charli said. She grinned. "After about three weeks of this!"

Leila frowned.

"Okay, one week of this," Charli compromised.

Leila shot her another look.

"Okay," Charli said. "Three days. And that's my final offer!"

Leila laughed, and Jami stood up to gaze at the sea, too.

"You know, we're lucky to be here at all," Leila said. "But I think I know why we are."

"Why?" Jami asked.

"Mr. Hammond has a thing for you."

"Oh, no," Jami said, shaking her head. "Mr. Hammond and I work together. There is no *thing*."

"Okay," Leila said. But she wasn't buying that.

"Mr. Hammond made that rule about not dating coworkers or employees or anything, right?" Charli asked Jami.

Jami nodded. "Yup."

Charli grinned. "Well, I think he wants to break his own rule."

"The way you'd like to break it to be with Paolo?" Jami asked with a smile.

Charli brushed her hair out of her face. "Okay, I admit it. I would have loved to get to know Paolo better. But it probably wouldn't have worked out, anyway. He thinks I'm a way too uptight American— and I think he's a way too laid-back Italian."

"Like oil and vinegar," Leila said.

"Well, I don't know about that," Jami said. "Oil and vinegar may not mix well. But put them on a salad and it's a great combination."

"I *do* love when Paolo mixes Italian and English," Charli said. "I mean, is he adorable or what?"

Jami smiled. "Maybe you'll get to spend more time with him."

"Really?" Charli's eyes lit up. "You mean we aren't being sent home?"

"Well, I don't know. But I told you not to call your parents yet for a reason," Jami said. "Derek Hammond has his own ideas about how to do things. Let's just see what he decides."

I'll keep my fingers crossed, Leila thought. But she didn't want to get her hopes up too much.

And besides—even if she *did* get her job back, how long would she be able to keep it? If Tortoni still had it in for her, he'd probably find a way to fire her—again!

I'll worry about that when the time comes, Leila decided. She picked up her camera. "I'm going down to take pictures on the beach," she announced.

"Well, have fun," Charli said, flopping back down into her lounge chair. "I'm getting all the exercise I need right here."

The beach wasn't as wide as the ones Leila was used to back home in L.A. But the water was a lot greener. And there was something almost magical about the light. Somehow it made everything seem...awesome.

She shot a whole roll of sand and water and dunes. Then she started hiking along a path near the water. Halfway down the trail, she bent to shoot some ferns.

All at once, an incredibly loud dune buggy roared toward her, almost plowing her over. It came to a screeching halt just a few yards from where she stood.

A guy in a surfer's wet suit jumped out of the dune buggy and rushed to see if she was okay.

"Are you nuts?" Leila shouted at him in English.

"Sorry. I didn't expect anyone would be here," he replied—in English! "There's usually no one around."

Leila frowned and checked him out quickly. Yeah, this guy was cute, all right. Green eyes, sun-bleached hair...he looked as if he was around seventeen years old. But there was something about him...something she instantly didn't like.

Maybe it was the cocky way he was grinning at her. He probably expected to get away with anything and everything—just because he was cute.

"It's okay," she said stiffly. "I'm fine." She paused, then decided to cut him some slack and introduce herself. "I'm Leila."

"I'm Ryan," he said.

"An American?" she asked.

The guy grinned. "Even better. A New Yorker."

That's what I didn't like, Leila thought. *He's totally full of himself.*

"Well, I'm from L.A.," she told him. "I'm staying at Mr. Hammond's villa for a few days. My sister and I are interning at his Hammond International."

"Hammond?" Ryan said. "Oh, I've heard of him. The big business dude who owns that fancy house."

"You got it," Leila said.

"Want to go for a ride?" Ryan asked, nodding toward his dune buggy.

Leila hesitated. She didn't really want to give this guy the satisfaction of going with him. But a ride did sound like a ton of fun....

"Sure," she said finally, climbing into the dune buggy. "Why not?"

"Don't worry," Ryan said. "I'll take it easy."

As soon as Leila was settled, Ryan gunned the engine. Then he ripped along the beach, bouncing along and kicking up sand the whole way.

This guy's an idiot, Leila thought. But she had to admit, the ride was totally-out-of-control fun.

Finally Ryan slammed on the brakes and came to a stop. "I didn't go too fast, did I?" he asked with a devilish grin.

"No," Leila lied. "I'm just glad I didn't eat lunch."

"Or you'd be wearing it?" he asked, looking extremely pleased with himself.

"No—*you'd* be wearing it," Leila said. She hopped out and motioned for him to switch places. "My turn to drive."

"You know how to drive one of these things?" Ryan asked, sounding surprised. But he moved over into the passenger seat to give Leila a chance.

"I'll learn," Leila told him. Then she gunned the engine and took off driving like an even bigger maniac than Ryan.

When she finally screeched to a stop, Ryan looked sick.

"I didn't go too fast now, did I?" she asked in a concerned voice.

"You're totally nuts!" Ryan shouted. He jumped out of the dune buggy and Leila did, too. "But I guess I deserved it," he added.

From behind them, a man's voice called out. "Ryan! What did I tell you about driving like that!"

Leila turned and saw Derek Hammond watching them from the road above them.

"Sorry, Uncle Derek," Ryan said. "It won't happen again."

Mr. Hammond nodded. Then he waved and walked away.

"Whoa. Hold on a sec," Leila said, frowning. "You're Derek Hammond's *nephew*?"

"I'm staying here for the summer," Ryan said.

"All by yourself?" Leila asked.

"I'm not alone," he said, sounding sort of defensive. "I've got my good buddies: Mr. Dune Buggy, Ms. Jet Ski, Uncle Harley Davidson…"

He's a beach bum, Leila thought. *How totally* not *original.*

"I'd be pretty bored if I were you," Leila said matter-of-factly.

Ryan grinned. "So, Leila from Los Angeles," he said, turning on all of his charm, "un-bore me."

"I'd prefer to un*load* you," she replied. She started to walk away.

"Hey, wait!" Ryan ran to catch up to her. "What's your problem? I thought you L.A. types were supposed to be laid back."

Laid-back? Leila thought. *There's a difference between being laid-back and being a total slacker.*

"My problem?" she said. "My problem is you're whacked."

For some reason, Ryan actually smiled when she said that. Did he think it was a compliment?

"Ryan, why aren't you in the intern program?" Leila asked. She figured she might as well make conversation. He was following her back toward the house.

Ryan's face clouded. "What is this, Twenty Questions?"

"No," Leila said, shrugging. "It's just that the intern program is in Rome. And you're very close to the city. I don't know, call me crazy…"

Ryan shook his head, looking disgusted. "I stick with sun and fun," he said. "Where's the bad in that?"

"Where's the bad?" Leila repeated. "Well, try this: You're all by yourself." Then she picked up her pace and left him behind in the sand.

CHAPTER EIGHT

"So was he cute?" Charli asked when Leila finished telling her all about Ryan.

"See for yourself," Leila said. She was standing by the window in their room at the villa, looking down toward the pool. "There he is."

Charli gazed out the window at the guy Leila pointed to. "Whoa, he's totally buff!" she said.

"Who cares?" Leila said. "He's also a jerk."

The two of them finished getting ready for dinner. Derek Hammond had made it clear that he wanted everyone to dress up. After sunset, they'd be having a fabulous meal, cooked by his personal staff and served at an elegant table by the pool.

"Welcome to the best hotel on earth," Ryan said as Leila and Charli joined everyone outside. "Just like the Hilton and the Hyatt. It's the Hammond."

Mr. Hammond grinned, but he seemed a little annoyed. As if he wanted to say, "My house is *not* a hotel—and only a spoiled brat would say so."

Instead, Derek Hammond turned to Leila and Charli. "I have some good news for you girls," Derek said. "I've talked to Mr. Tortoni. You're both being given a second chance."

"We are?" Leila cried. "Oh, thank you, Mr. Hammond! Thank you so much!"

"You won't regret it," Charli promised.

"I'm sure I won't," Mr. Hammond said. "But let me give you a bit of advice...."

"What?" Leila asked eagerly.

Mr. Hammond glanced at Jami across the table and his eyes twinkled. "Remember the seven C's?" he asked her. "All those years ago?"

"You mean when I was a twenty-year-old college intern and you were just starting your business at the age of twenty-five?" Jami asked.

Mr. Hammond nodded. "Jami was my first intern," he told the others. "And I came up with this list—my seven C's. Be clever, be conscientious, be calm, be consistent, be cooperative, be creative, and most importantly, be confident."

"It worked," Jami said. "Look where it got you."

"Where it got *us*," Mr. Hammond said, staring at her with a special meaning in his eyes.

They are *in love*, Leila thought. And they'd known each other for years! So why didn't they just go for it?

"Enough about business," Jami said quickly. "I'm going to check out the night sky."

"Why don't you all do some astronomy," Mr. Hammond said. "I'd like to talk to Leila for a minute. Alone."

Leila gulped. Why did he want to talk to *her*?

When Jami, Charli, and Ryan were out of earshot, Mr. Hammond lowered his voice and looked Leila straight in the eyes.

"I have a favor to ask you," he said. "You see, I invited my nephew Ryan here this summer for a reason—to interest him in the internship program."

"What's your plan B?" Leila asked.

"You're quick." Mr. Hammond smiled. "Plan B was inviting you and Charli to the beach, hoping he would connect with you girls and want to give work a try."

"What's plan C?" Leila asked.

Mr. Hammond's shoulders slumped. "Actually, I was hoping you might have a plan C," he admitted.

Leila thought about the situation. Ryan was a hard case. He seemed really determined to slack off for the rest of eternity.

But I owe Mr. Hammond big time, she thought. *Especially now that he's gotten me my job back.*

"Give me a little time," she told Mr. Hammond. "I promise I'll come up with something."

"Thanks," Mr. Hammond said. "I'm sure you will. Excuse me." He got up and left the table to join Jami on the terrace.

So what do I do now? Leila wondered. How could she possibly get Ryan interested in a job in Rome when he'd rather be here, hanging out all day?

Ryan came up beside her. "So Leila, it looks like I won't see you anymore after Sunday," he said.

"I'm totally psyched that we're going back to work," Leila said. "It's a lot of fun. And there's tons of stuff to learn about fashion."

"Well, I'm totally bummed you're leaving," Ryan said. "I admit it."

"So come with us," Leila urged him, looking into his eyes. "Work for your Uncle D. You'd love it, if you just gave it a try."

He ignored her and leaned in close with his eyes closed.

No way, Leila told him silently. *Don't even try to kiss me.* Even though Ryan was cute, Leila didn't want to get involved with a guy who was only interested in ways to blow off responsibilities and avoid real life. She moved away slightly.

"That was going to be for good-bye," Ryan said, sounding hurt.

No thanks, she thought. *There just aren't any sparks with a guy I can't respect.*

"Let's go hang with the others." Leaving Ryan at the table, Leila walked quickly to the edge of the terrace and gazed up at the stars.

What am I going to do? she wondered. *I promised Derek Hammond I'd help out with Ryan, but I'm already failing miserably.*

And when she headed back to Rome, there would be another huge problem waiting for her.

A problem named Tortoni.

CHAPTER NINE

"Heidi actually *apologized*?" Charli said. Her mouth dropped open. "You're kidding."

Leila and Charli had been back in Rome on the job all morning. So far, things were going amazingly well. Now they were sitting in a café, eating lunch and talking about Heidi.

"Well no, she didn't exactly apologize," Leila said, shaking her head. "But she's has been acting a lot nicer. I guess Nobu ragged on her, while we were gone, for lying to Mr. Tortoni about the CD. She must have taken it to heart."

"Amazing," Charli said, sipping her Limonato soda.

Leila took a bite of her delicious sandwich made with prosciutto, a thin slice of cheese, and arugula.

"So, are you using the seven C's?" Charli asked.

"I'm trying," Leila said. "Dari and I are definitely being creative. We put on Rollerblades to speed up the mail delivery. What about you?"

"I borrowed a Global Positioning System from Ryan before we left," Charli said. "Paolo and I are using it to find our way around Rome. We finished three hours' worth of deliveries in one hour this morning."

"Awesome!" Leila said. "How's it going with

Paolo anyway? What have you guys been up to?"

Charli groaned. "Don't ask. I'm using the eighth C when it comes to him. Cheating!"

"You're cheating on Paolo?" Leila's eyes widened in shock. "I thought you really liked him!"

"I do!" Charli said. "I mean, I'm cheating on Mr. Hammond's 'no dating among the interns' rule."

Leila shook her head. "Just don't get caught. We can't afford to make any more mistakes on this job."

"I know." Charli sighed. "I don't want Tortoni to bust me for being with Paolo—but I just like him so much!"

"What do you like about him?" Leila asked.

Charli shrugged. "I can't explain it, really. At first I thought he wasn't taking this job seriously. But the more I talk to him, the more I get the feeling that he has something else he totally cares about. Some secret passion. I just haven't found out what it is."

Leila glanced at her watch. "Speaking of being busted by Tortoni, we'd better get back. Lunch hour is over." She jumped up from the table and started back toward the Hammond offices. "Aren't you coming?" she called over her shoulder to Charli.

Charli shook her head. "Uh, Paolo and I have a few more deliveries to make," she said with a grin.

"Yeah, right," Leila answered. "Like I said—just don't get caught!" She hurried back to the mail room to see if there was anything new going on.

"A few letters came in by hand for Jami," Dari told her.

"I'll take them to her," Leila offered. She zoomed off on her Rollerblades toward Jami's corner office.

When she arrived there, she found the office full of people: designers, two models, a seamstress, and Mr. Tortoni.

Leila hovered near the entrance, watching and listening. Everyone seemed to be arguing over the hem length on a new dress design.

"Higher," Jami said. "At least an inch."

At least two inches, Leila thought. She wouldn't be caught dead in that dress the way the hemline was now.

The seamstress started to fold the hemline up, but one of the designers stopped her. "No, the hem is just right," he said. "Mr. Tortoni thinks it's perfect this way. Am I right, signor?"

"Yes," Mr. Tortoni said. "That hemline is correct. No shorter, please."

"Wait," a commanding voice behind Leila said. "Don't you think you should ask your future customers first?"

Everyone in the office looked up to see who was interfering. Leila whirled around. Derek Hammond was standing behind her.

"Hello, Leila," he said, glancing at her Rollerblades. "Very innovative. I like that."

"Thanks, Mr. Hammond," Leila said.

"Good afternoon, Derek," Mr. Tortoni said. "I didn't expect to see you today." His lips suddenly looked tight.

"Excuse my interruption," Mr. Hammond said, "but we do have one of our future customers standing right here. Don't you think you should ask her opinion?"

Mr. Tortoni frowned.

"Leila? What do you think of this outfit?" Mr. Hammond asked.

"Nice," Leila answered, trying to be diplomatic.

"No," Mr. Hammond said. "I want the truth, please."

"Yes, Signorina Hunter," Mr. Tortoni said. "Do enlighten us."

"Well, okay." Leila nodded. "Your target customer is eighteen to thirty years old. Young, stylish, carefree, and hip. But these clothes seem geared to an older woman. Which is fine—it's just not your target."

"Raise the hem *two* inches!" one of the designers declared.

Mr. Hammond and Jami both nodded and smiled.

The models cheered, and Leila beamed—until she caught Mr. Tortoni's face. He was glaring at her, as if she'd done something totally wrong again.

Why? Because she'd voted for a shorter hemline? Or was he just annoyed because she'd challenged him—and kind of made him look bad in front of Derek Hammond?

Or...was it something even more than that?

Suddenly she remembered the phone conversation she'd overheard—with Tortoni promising someone that he'd get the designs before the fashion shoot.

Hmmm. If the hemlines changed, that might spoil Tortoni's plans—whatever they were.

Maybe it's time to find out what he's up to, Leila decided as she skated back to the mail room. *Once and for all.*

She turned down the aisle toward Mr. Tortoni's office. Something told her that Tortoni *wanted* the upcoming photo shoot to fail. And if so, didn't she owe it to Derek Hammond to find out why?

This was a perfect time to dig up some evidence. Everyone was gathered in Jami's office, working on the designs.

She waited to make sure no one was coming. Then she slipped into Mr. Tortoni's office and began searching his desk.

Fashion designs, spreadsheets with numbers, memos, e-mails, fabric samples, CDs, reports...

Then she saw it: an envelope from a company called Runaway Threads.

I've heard of them! Leila realized. She'd seen something on TV last year about a company that copied big-name designer clothes—and sold them dirt cheap.

What's Tortoni doing with mail from *them*? she wondered.

She leaned closer to read a handwritten note that was scrawled on the envelope. Most of it was in Italian. The only words she recognized were *camicetta* and *pantaloni*—which meant blouse and pants. Then she saw a money amount: 40,000 euros.

Underneath it, in English, someone had scrawled, "Half now, half on delivery of the designs."

Oh, man. What's going on here? Leila wondered. *Is Tortoni betraying Derek Hammond and selling his hot new designs to Runaway Threads?*

Just then she heard voices in the hall. Someone was coming!

Leila's heart pounded. She skated out of the office as fast as she could. Then she turned left and took the long way around, hoping that Mr. Tortoni wouldn't see her.

She zoomed back toward the mail room. But as she rounded the corner, she gasped.

Mr. Tortoni was standing right there at the copy machine!

Leila froze. Unless her eyes were fooling her, Mr. Tortoni was copying the newest design sketches from the spring show!

CHAPTER TEN

"Is that unbelievable or what?" Leila said after she'd told the whole story to Charli a few hours later. "I caught Tortoni red-handed—stealing the new Hammond designs!"

"And he didn't even flinch when you saw him? He just *stood* there?" Charli asked.

"No, he flinched," Leila explained. "He looked *totally* guilty. But he covered everything up pretty well by asking me to put the copies on Jami's desk."

"Did you tell Jami what happened?" Charli asked.

"She was already gone for the day," Leila explained. "So was Mr. Hammond."

"Well, that sounds like pretty good proof," Charli said. "But is it really? I mean, all you saw was an envelope with some numbers and words on it. You don't even know who wrote them."

Leila flopped down on their big bed in the palazzo. "I know. I should have taken the envelope or something to show Jami. Or Mr. Hammond."

"Well, maybe that envelope from Runaway Threads was from a business letter," Charli said. "You can't be sure that Tortoni is working for them."

"You don't think I should tell Jami?" Leila asked.

"Not until you have definite proof," Charli said. "And I'd be really careful until then, especially if you think Tortoni is out to get you. Besides, Jami isn't here right now."

"I know. I think she and Mr. Hammond cut out early from work together," Leila said.

Charli smiled. "Excellent! The two of them seem like a perfect couple, don't they?"

Leila nodded. "They do."

"And if *they're* going out, then maybe Mr. Hammond won't get on my case for dating Paolo," Charli went on. "So—what should I wear tonight?"

She reached into the tall armoire and pulled out two outfits. One was a pair of red capris with a boat-neck top. The other was a black cotton dress.

"The dress," Leila advised. "It's better for evening."

"Are you sure you don't mind staying here all alone tonight?" Charli asked. "I mean, Nobu, Dari, and Heidi are already checking out the lights in Piazza del Popolo. You should have gone with them."

"I'm okay," Leila said. "I'm going to clean my camera."

Charli rolled her eyes. "That's got to be the lamest way to spend a summer night in Rome I've ever heard. Why don't you come out with Paolo and me? It will be fun."

Leila smiled. "I'll be fine."

Charli sighed. She hated to leave Leila alone.

But Paolo was ready to go. She couldn't cancel now. "Okay, if you're sure," she said. "See you later."

"Have fun," Leila called after her.

Paolo was waiting for Charli downstairs in the foyer. When he saw her coming, he gave her a huge grin. *"Bellissima!"* he said, taking her hand.

"So where are we going?" she asked as they headed outside.

"Remember today when you asked me why I wasn't into the internship program?" Paolo said.

Charli nodded.

"Tonight I show you why," he said.

Paolo held her hand tightly, and pulled her a little closer as they walked. Charli felt her skin tingle.

"Come on, tell me," she said. "Where are we going?"

"You'll see," he answered mysteriously, approaching a Vespa. "Climb on."

Gladly, Charli thought as she snuggled close to Paolo on the motorbike.

The stars twinkled brightly overhead as they made their way through the narrow streets.

Finally Paolo pulled up at a small restaurant with an outdoor patio strung with tiny white lights. He took Charli by the hand again and led her inside—all the way into the kitchen in the back.

"Welcome to Scalini's," Paolo said. "My family's restaurant. This is my passion. This is what I want to do."

Wow, Charli thought. He sounded so sincere, so committed. He was like a totally different person the minute he'd stepped into this place.

"If you want to be a chef, why did you join the internship program?" she asked.

"It was my father's and grandfather's idea," Paolo said. "Their dream, not mine. Mr. Hammond likes to eat here, so they asked him to take me. They have both been chefs. They think it is no future for me. But I do not agree."

With a proud smile, Paolo took Charli around the kitchen and introduced her to everyone. His gray-haired grandmother sat in a chair in the back. His mother was sewing in a nearby alcove.

This is so sweet! Charli thought. She loved seeing how much Paolo cared about his family.

Paolo tied an apron around Charli's waist. "Come," he said. "I teach you to make pizza dough."

"*Grazie*," Charli said, using the Italian word for "thank you."

Paolo leaned over and showed her how to knead the dough. Charli was impressed by how carefully he did it—until it was just right.

Then it was time to toss the dough in the air and catch it.

"I don't know about this," Charli said. "Should I?"

"Yes," Paolo said. "Like this." He demonstrated a perfect toss.

61

"Okay, here goes," Charli said. She tossed the dough up in the air, but not very high.

In the corner, Paolo's mother and grandmother laughed and chattered in Italian.

"Are they making fun of me?" Charli asked.

"Just do it," Paolo instructed her. "Again!"

"Okay." She tossed the dough as hard as she could, trying to spin it in a circle at the same time. But it flew out of her hands like a Frisbee and sailed up to the ceiling. "Oh, no!" Charli covered her mouth with her hand, getting flour all over her face.

They all stared up at the ceiling. The dough was stuck up there, and it wasn't coming down.

"No problem," Paolo said. "We share *my* pizza, and I make us pasta *pomodoro*."

Twenty minutes later, the two of them sat down at a candlelit table on the patio. The pizza and one large bowl of pasta were between them.

"This is delicious," Charli said, putting a forkful of pasta in her mouth. "You're a great chef."

"*Grazie*," Paolo said.

"My pizza dough, on the other hand, is now a ceiling tile!" Charli joked.

Paolo grinned. "Who said, 'What goes up must come down'? They don't know Charli Hunter!"

"True!" Charli giggled. Then she grew serious. "But, really, Paolo, now I can understand why you don't care so much about the internship."

Hi, I'm Leila Hunter. My sister, Charli, and I have cool summer jobs at a famous fashion house—in Italy!

I love to explore Rome with my camera. There's so much to see!

Here we are
on the Spanish
Steps, having
fun with our
new friends!

Looks like Charli
even has a
crush on one of
them. His name
is Paolo.

And guess what? Paolo likes her, too!

But then I get fired from my job for messing up a delivery...

And Charli gets fired for making bad coffee.
It's not long before all our friends are fired, too!

I find out we were set up by the boss! And I use my camera to prove it!

We all get our jobs back.
The gang is reunited!

Well, we've got to run to work now. Ciao!

"Really?" he asked.

"Yes," Charli said. "And if this is what you want to do with your life, you should do it."

Paolo's eyes locked with hers. What could she say? He was just about the sweetest, nicest, most charming guy she'd met in a long time.

She smiled shyly as Paolo leaned a little closer to her. Then she leaned in closer to him. Soon, they were almost kissing. *Go on,* Charli thought. *Kiss me.*

She and Paolo both looked around, to see if anyone was watching.

A few tables away, Mr. Hammond and Jami were having dinner together under the stars.

Whoa, Charli thought. That definitely wasn't a business dinner. Mr. Hammond and Jami were kissing, too! "Look," she said softly.

Paolo followed her gaze.

At that instant, Hammond and Jami glanced up and saw Paolo's mouth an inch away from Charli's.

Oh, well, Charli thought. *At least we're* all *busted!*

She smiled sheepishly at Jami.

Jami waved back, but Mr. Hammond jumped up quickly, looking very uncomfortable.

What now? Charli worried. Was he going to fire her for breaking the rules and dating an intern—when he was doing exactly the same thing himself?

CHAPTER ELEVEN

Okay, so I lied, Leila thought.

She was sitting in the dark palazzo all alone, putting the lens back on her camera.

I lied about wanting to stay home alone. Who knew it was going to be so dark and creepy in here?

The soft lights from the street streamed in the tall palazzo windows, creating shadows on the walls. But the two small sconces on the wall gave off almost no light.

Suddenly something outside made a huge bang.

"Who's there?" Leila called out, her heart pounding. She tiptoed slowly toward the door.

No answer.

Leila took another step—just one—toward the door. "Is someone here?" she called.

Almost immediately, the door swung open. "Surprise!" a guy's voice called. The person stepped into the foyer and held up a key. Ryan!

"Surprise? Try heart failure!" Leila snapped. "What are you doing here?" she demanded.

"Uncle D owns this place," Ryan said with a cocky smile. "So I borrowed a key and took the train up. I thought maybe we could go out."

No way, Leila thought. *This guy thinks he's so hot, he can just drop in here on a Friday night without warning, and I'll be sitting around with nothing better to do?*

Who cared if it was true...?

"Sorry," she said, turning back to her camera. "No thanks."

Ryan's voice softened a little. "I know you don't have much respect for me," he said, "and you think I'm kind of lazy..."

Leila shot him a look that said: Right on both counts.

"But it's Rome," Ryan rushed on. "And it's summer, and we both have nothing to do."

Those are valid points, Leila thought. But if she went out with him, he'd get the wrong idea. He'd think she was interested in him—and she wasn't.

"Sorry," Leila said again.

Ryan's shoulders sank. "What if I take you for the best gelato on earth?" he asked.

Well, at least he's working pretty hard at this, Leila thought, starting to soften a little. *And it* would *be nice to get out of there.*

"Well, okay," Leila finally gave in. "I guess I could use some fresh air."

The two of them strolled down Via di Ripetta toward a gelato place near the Piazza Navona. The line outside was about twenty people long.

"I guess a few other people know about this

place," Leila said as they waited their turn to order.

"Do you have a favorite ice cream?" Ryan asked.

"No. I have about five favorites," Leila said.

"Well then, you've come to the right country," Ryan said. "You can get three or four different flavors in one cup here."

"Really? That rocks!" Leila smiled at him for the first time.

When they reached the front of the line, Leila got a taste of three flavors: melon, coffee, and blueberry.

They walked back toward the Spanish Steps, eating their gelato. "Listen, Leila, I've got to ask you something," Ryan began.

But Leila was only half listening.

Down the block, she saw someone talking to two guys who looked as if they had walked out of a gangster movie. He had the same black-rimmed glasses and bald head as Mr. Tortoni. Could it be him?

"I um...need to know something," Ryan said.

Leila frowned. It was Tortoni, all right.

"Are you listening to me?" Ryan asked.

"Huh?" Leila replied.

Tortoni was handing one of the men a thick envelope. It was too small to have sketches in it. It looked more like an envelope full of cash.

Then all three men glanced over their shoulders, as if they wanted to make sure no one saw them.

That's weird, Leila thought. Why was Tortoni paying *them*? She'd figured Runaway Threads was going to pay Tortoni.

"Leila?" Ryan stopped walking and stood in front of her.

"What?" she asked, turning her gaze away from Tortoni. "Sorry. What were you saying?"

"Be honest," Ryan said. "Why don't you like me?"

"I like you," Leila said carefully. *Just not that much*, she added silently.

"No come on, really," Ryan said.

Leila sighed. "You want the truth?" she asked.

He nodded.

She looked at her watch. "Sorry, but I have to be back in two hours. There's not enough time to tell you."

"Ouch!" Ryan said, looking hurt. "Am I that bad?"

"Look, I don't mean to be harsh," Leila said. She softened her voice a little. "But your uncle would be so happy if you joined the internship program. Or even if you did something—anything—more challenging than applying SPF 25 all day."

Ryan shook his head in disgust. "No way," he said. "I know that's the real reason why Uncle Derek invited me to Italy. He wants to instill some sort of work ethic in me. But I am never going to be like him."

"So you mean it's not worth trying?" Leila asked.

Ryan seemed frustrated, as if he wanted her to understand. "Look, see that gelato?" he said, pointing to the ground. "It's the best, right? But if it was my family's business, I wouldn't get involved— because I could never do better."

"Then try something else," Leila said. "Like making Jell-O."

"Hey, I'm seventeen," Ryan argued. "I've got my whole life ahead of me. Cut me some slack."

"Fine," Leila said. "Stay home at the beach and play with your uncle's toys all summer."

Just don't expect me to join you, she added silently. *I have better things to do, like find out what Tortoni is up to—and stop him. But how?*

"Listen," she said to Ryan. "I have an idea about something important I need to do. But I may need some help. Can I count on you?"

Ryan shrugged. "I don't know. Maybe."

Leila put her hands on her hips. "Do you want my respect or not?"

Ryan hesitated. "Well, yeah. I guess."

"What about some respect for yourself?" Leila added. "That's even more important."

"Okay," Ryan said. "I'll help you. As long as it doesn't involve joining the internship program."

Leila nodded. "Fine. It's a deal."

CHAPTER TWELVE

"Good morning, interns," Mr. Tortoni said the next day. "I have an important job for all of you today—and a surprise."

I don't like his surprises, Leila thought uneasily. *Is this some big plan he cooked up last night?*

"In three days, we have the fashion magazine photo shoot," Mr. Tortoni went on. "But first the clothing must be cleaned. The cleaners is only a short way, so you will walk it there. Wait for the clothes. Then bring them back to the office."

Nobu shot Leila and the others a puzzled look. "But these clothes have never been worn," he said. "They're all new—just made."

Mr. Tortoni glared at him. "You question me?"

"I just mean, do you trust these cleaners?" Nobu asked. "What if they ruin the clothes?"

"Too much worrying," Mr. Tortoni said, sounding annoyed. Then he put on a gracious smile. "But since you all did a great job yesterday, I am treating you to lunch. The café is on the way to the cleaners, so you will go there first. Everything has been taken care of. Here is the address. Go, eat, enjoy."

As the interns began to leave the room, Leila

pulled Charli aside. "Listen, I'm not coming with you. Ryan and I have something to do," she whispered.

"What's up?" Charli asked.

"I can't tell you now," Leila said. "But involves Tortoni. I'll catch up with you later."

"Okay," Charli said. "But be careful."

"I will," Leila promised. "And don't worry—I won't get us fired again. Trust me on that!"

"Where are Paolo and Leila?" Nobu asked as the interns pushed the rack of clothing out of the Hammond offices.

"Paolo's making a delivery," Charli explained. "And Leila...uh, already had plans for lunch."

"Smart girl," Heidi said bitterly. "*She's* not pushing clothes through the streets of Rome."

"Well, that *is* part of our job," Charli said.

"You have such a great attitude," Dari told Charli. "You and Leila will get picked to go to New York, for sure."

"Yes, but just because the two of them are Hammond's beach house buddies," Heidi said.

"No—because they're the best interns," Nobu said.

It was nice to know Charli had the respect of her fellow interns. Most of them, anyway.

She wished Heidi would drop the bad attitude and get with the team. Sure, Heidi had *tried* to be nicer lately, but honestly, it wasn't working.

They reached the restaurant near the cleaners. The four of them sat down at a table outside.

"*Buongiorno.*" The maître d' approached them. "You must be Signor Tortoni's special people. He has arranged everything. The antipasti buffet is inside." He motioned for them to follow him.

All four interns started to go inside.

"Wait!" Charli said suddenly. "We can't just leave the clothes out here, unattended."

"I will keep them safe for you," the maître d' announced. "Don't worry."

"Great," Nobu replied. "Thanks." He turned to Dari and offered his arm. "Shall we?" he asked.

Dari giggled as the two walked inside.

"They make a cute couple, don't you think?" Charli said to Heidi as they followed Dari and Nobu into the café.

"I guess." Heidi frowned.

"What's wrong?" Charli demanded. "Why can't you loosen up a little bit and just enjoy life?"

Whoa, she thought immediately. She sounded just like Paolo!

"Loosen up?" Heidi put her hands on her hips. "What's the point? You and Leila will never treat me the way you treat the others."

"What do you mean?" Charli asked.

"You would do anything for your friends," Heidi said. "But not for me."

"Hey—we'd do anything for anyone who's part of our *team*," Charli said. "That's what being a good friend is all about, if you ask me."

Heidi hesitated. Then she nodded, as if she wanted to get on board with that idea. Maybe she just wasn't sure how, Charli realized.

"Whatever," Heidi said. But she gave Charli a tiny smile.

"Hey, look," Charli said as the two of them returned to the patio. "Dari and Nobu are kissing." She cleared her throat. "Ahh-hemm."

Nobu pulled away from Dari. "Hey, the food looks good," he said, sounding slightly embarrassed.

Charli glanced around. "Wait a minute," she said. "What happened to the clothes?"

"I bet the maitre d' took them," Heidi replied.

"I'm going to check on them, just to make sure," Charli said. She headed inside the restaurant. But the maître d' was nowhere to be found. She even tried describing him to one of the other waiters.

"Sorry, signorina," the waiter replied. "No one with that description works here."

Charli's stomach started to turn. The maître d'— and the whole rolling rack of clothes—had disappeared! All the Hammond fashions for the new spring line!

CHAPTER THIRTEEN

"This is just not possible," Charli said, slumping to the floor back at the palazzo. "I've been fired twice in two days. And Leila's going to totally freak when she hears that she's been canned, too!"

"It's so unfair," Dari said, shaking her head. "Leila and Paolo weren't even there when the clothes got stolen. How could Tortoni fire them?"

Good question, Charli thought. But she had an idea about the answer. It had to have something to do with the sneaky deal Tortoni was pulling. *And* the fact that Leila was onto him.

Where was her sister, anyway?

"It's so unfair," Dari repeated.

Dari and Nobu sat cross-legged on the floor in the foyer. Charli took out her sketchpad from her knapsack and started to draw. Somehow, sketching always made her feel better.

"I guess we should all be packing," Dari said glumly. "But I just hate to leave."

"Well, my flight to Munich leaves in two hours," Heidi said as she rolled her suitcase into the foyer.

"Of course." Nobu made a face. "Rats are always the first to leave a sinking ship."

Charli winced. Couldn't Nobu see that Heidi had been trying to shape up?

Jami hurried in from the kitchen and glanced at Heidi's packed bag.

"Jami, can't we just call Derek?" Charli asked. "He'll know what to do."

Jami shook her head. "Derek hired us for a reason—because he believes in us. *We* are going to figure out how to save the fashion shoot. There are only three more days left. We can't just give up."

"But there *is* no fashion shoot," Charli pointed out. "The clothes were stolen, remember?"

Jami gave them all a confident smile. "Remember what Derek—I mean, Mr. Hammond—always says. Be confident, calm, clever, *creative*..." She lifted the sketchpad off Charle's lap.

Oh, no, Charli thought. *No way. If she's thinking what I* think *she's thinking...she's nuts!*

"We'll make our own clothes," Jami said. "And when Fillitti gets here, we'll do our own shoot!"

"Jami, that's a great idea, but it's...uh, delusional," Nobu said.

"I am *not* crazy," Jami insisted. "We can do this, guys!" She looked at all the interns pleadingly.

Charli thought about it. The plan *was* pretty crazy—but what did they have to lose? "We could try, I guess," she said.

"I'm up for it," Nobu announced.

"Then I'm in, too," Dari said with a nod.

Everyone turned to Heidi.

"I'm going to miss my flight," Heidi said, looking at the ground. "And besides"—she hesitated—"no one really wants me here, anyway."

Jami's voice softened. "Heidi, if you were a little nicer to people, they might feel differently."

Heidi swallowed hard.

Come on, Charli told her silently. *Say it.*

"I'm sorry for being...you know...a jerk," Heidi said in a tiny voice. She didn't look at any of them.

"Great," Charli said. "Now all you need to do is tell that to Leila."

"Are you guys talking about me?" Leila walked in from the back door with Ryan behind her.

Jami's mouth dropped open when she saw Ryan. "What are *you* doing here?"

"Working," he said. He actually sounded proud.

"You?" Charli blurted out.

"Miracles happen," he said with a shrug. "For the right cause."

"Leila, I'm glad you're here," Jami said quickly. "A lot has happened. We need to produce our own fashion line using Charli's designs. And we don't have much time."

"Because the real clothes are missing and we were all fired?" Leila guessed.

"How did you know that?" Heidi asked.

Leila turned to Charli. "I told you I thought Tortoni was acting weird ever since we got here. So today Ryan and I conducted our own investigation and took some pictures. Here's the proof!"

Ryan pulled a stack of photos out of an envelope he was holding and spread them around on the floor.

Charli leaned forward for a closer look. All the other interns crowded around, too.

The pictures told an amazing story. The first few were shots of Charli, Dari, Nobu, and Heidi walking with the rack of clothing.

Then came a shot of Mr. Tortoni with two men, following the interns in a truck.

"I saw Tortoni giving those men an envelope last night," Leila explained. "I figured he was paying them to do *something* bad. So I decided to find out what."

Next was a picture of the maitre d' standing next to the clothing rack in front of the café.

Then Leila showed them a shot of the two men getting out of the truck, and the maitre d' helping them steal the clothes!

"We followed Tortoni and the clothes to this warehouse," Leila said, dropping another photo on the floor. "It belongs to Runaway Threads. Tortoni is selling Hammond's designs to a knockoff company."

Jami shook her head. "I'm totally impressed."

"And that's not all," Leila went on. "From what

Ryan and I overheard, Tortoni has been ripping off the company for years."

Charli looked at her sister in admiration.

"But this time Tortoni's gone way too far," Leila added. "He's trying to embarrass Mr. Hammond in front of Fillitti and the whole fashion world."

"That would be a disaster." Jami frowned. "It took us two years to convince Fillitti that Hammond designs are good enough for him to photograph."

"We can't let that disaster happen," Ryan said. "But how do we stop it?"

"Well, whatever we do, I want to tell Leila I'm sorry," Heidi said.

Leila nodded. "No problem," she said.

"But what about the photo shoot?" Charli asked.

"We've still got your designs," Jami told her.

Charli threw her sister a questioning glance. Was this whole idea way too crazy, or what?

"It's a long shot," Leila said slowly. "But it's all we've got. Mr. Hammond believed in us and gave us a second chance. So let's do something to help *him*—if we can."

Ryan stepped forward. "You heard Leila," he said. "Let's quit goofing around and get to work! *Pronto!*"

Wow! Charli thought. *If Ryan can get that pumped up about something, so can we!*

This plan just might work. It had to.

CHAPTER FOURTEEN

"What time is it?" Dari mumbled sleepily.

"Two-twenty," Jami answered with a yawn. "In the *morning*."

Leila gazed around the foyer of the palazzo. It was amazing. They were actually doing it! There was fabric spread out everywhere. Dari, Heidi, and Leila were cutting. Paolo's mother and grandmother had set up their sewing machines in a corner, and were busily sewing away. Jami and Charli were pinning the new clothes on two models they'd hired. Nobu was making lists, and Ryan was running errands every time they needed scissors, more thread, sequins, or whatever.

"We have to get something to eat," Nobu said from his spot on the floor.

"Forget food," Ryan said. "We have a job to do."

Talk about a total turnaround! Leila thought.

But even if they all kept pulling together, they couldn't go on like this for another day. They hadn't slept in thirty-six hours.

"Ryan, chill," Leila said. "Let me explain the world of work to you: You're allowed to take breaks!"

"And eat," Heidi reminded Leila. "Please tell him

that you're allowed to eat. I'm totally starving!"

"Don't worry about food," Charli said. "It's under control."

A minute later, Paolo raced in with three pizza boxes under his arms. His mother and grandmother smiled from the corner.

"*Ciao*, Paolo!" they called.

"I've got two Charlis and one *cipolle e acciughe*," Paolo announced.

"What's a Charli?" Leila asked.

"It's a pizza he invented," Charli explained. "He named it after me. It has asparagus, arugula, and three kinds of cheese. My favorites."

"What's the other one?" Heidi asked.

"Uh, onions and anchovies," Charli said.

"I'll take a slice of Charli," Leila muttered.

"Me, too," Dari called.

"Give me a Charli," Nobu, Jami, and Heidi all said.

Paolo laughed and grinned at his grandmother. "See, *Nonna*? All the more *cipolle e acciughe* for you and me."

By dawn, Leila was having a hard time keeping her eyes open. She yawned and curled up on some pillows in the foyer. Dari, Heidi, and Nobu were already sacked out on the floor. They'd been sleeping for the past two hours. Only Ryan was still working.

At least we got most of Charli's designs put together, Leila thought as she drifted off to sleep.

The sound of footsteps on the marble floor made her open her eyes. What now? Was Tortoni sneaking in here to steal Charli's designs, too? She raised her head and squinted through the morning light.

It was Derek Hammond!

Leila sat up and watched as Mr. Hammond took in the scene in his palazzo foyer. Fabric was scattered everywhere. Five mannequins stood draped with new designs. The floor was littered with sleeping interns, pins, scissors, pizza boxes, Charli's sketches, Leila's pictures, and three days' worth of empty drink cups. It was a total mess.

Hammond stared at Ryan as if he were looking at a ghost. "What are *you* doing here?" he asked.

"Everyone always asks me that," Ryan said. "I'm working. For Hammond International. Sort of."

Mr. Hammond walked over and messed up Ryan's hair, grinning affectionately. "I knew I'd be proud of you one day."

Ryan grinned back. "Okay, everybody up!" he called. "Today's the shoot!"

All at once, Leila felt wide awake. They'd actually done it! They'd pulled off a miracle—and now Charli's fashions were about to be shot by one of the most famous photographers in the world.

"Ryan, you're nuts," Heidi said groggily.

"I think I created a monster," Leila said as she jumped to her feet.

"I guess we found plan C," Mr. Hammond said, winking at Leila.

When Charli realized that Mr. Hammond was there, she jumped up, too.

"Charli, your designs are exquisite." Mr. Hammond said. He stared at the clothes draped on the mannequins.

Charli beamed. "Thank you, sir."

Yes! Leila thought. She was so happy for her sister. Mr. Hammond had noticed her talent!

"Derek, I have something to show you," Jami said. She started to gather up the photos.

Mr. Hammond waved a hand. "I've known about Tortoni for several years," he said. "Or, rather, I knew he was doing some minor things. But he's been with me since I started the business. He almost feels like a partner. I guess I felt a sense of loyalty toward him. I kept giving him a chance to shape up and come clean. But from the looks of your pictures, Leila, he's gone too far this time."

"Way too far, Mr. Hammond," Charli said. "He stole the whole spring collection."

"Do you still feel loyal to him now?" Jami asked.

"No," Mr. Hammond said firmly.

"All right!" Ryan declared, shooting a fist in the air. "Let's take that weasel down!"

Mr. Hammond nodded in agreement. "But first, we've got to get ready for the shoot," he said.

Leila, Charli, and their friends sprang into action and finished the last of the designs. Then they packed up everything for the photo shoot, hopped into taxis, and drove to the Spanish Steps.

They were just in time. Fillitti, the great fashion photographer, was waiting for them impatiently. "I need more assistants!" he exclaimed. "You will help me," he said, pointing at Leila and Ryan.

Leila was so excited, she actually felt dizzy!

For the next few hours, she loaded film while Ryan helped Fillitti set up lights. Then Fillitti started photographing the models—and Charli's designs!

"This is so cool," Ryan said when Leila came back for more film.

"Better than your toys back home?" she asked.

"Maybe. But not better than you." He leaned over to kiss her.

Leila playfully pulled out of Ryan's reach and giggled.

Fillitti caught them out of the corner of his eyes. "*Amore* later," he said. "Working, now!"

Everyone laughed, including Mr. Hammond.

Leila pulled away and handed Fillitti a newly loaded camera. Then Fillitti went back to shooting the models.

"Well," Mr. Hammond said. "It seems my team

has done a great job. And here comes your payoff."

Leila followed his gaze and saw Mr. Tortoni walking toward them through a courtyard.

"What is *he* doing here?" Charli blurted out.

"Don't worry, Charli," Mr. Hammond said. "I called him myself."

"Derek!" Mr. Tortoni said, trying to act superfriendly. "I'm so glad you called. The shoot looks terrific. As you know, such an unfortunate thing happened—all the clothes disappeared. Vanished. And I, in the heat of the moment, blamed the interns. But it's really no one's fault."

"Oh, yes it is," Mr. Hammond said. "It's *your* fault, Enrico. I know what you did."

"Derek, what do you mean?" Mr. Tortoni tried to act innocent. "*Me?*"

Mr. Hammond stared at his old friend, his face filled with disappointment. "We have proof, Enrico."

Mr. Tortoni's face fell. Then he threw up his hands. "Twelve years of living in your shadow," he said bitterly. "You got all the glory...you got the girl"—he glanced at Jami, his eyes jealous and angry—"and I got—"

"A lot," Mr. Hammond replied, "and then you got greedy."

The two of them stared at each other again.

"So are you going to fire me?" Mr. Tortoni asked.

"I'm having you arrested," Mr. Hammond replied.

Yes! Leila thought. She felt like dancing around the courtyard.

"The police are expecting you at the station," Hammond went on, "and I've arranged a car to take you there." He pointed to a black limousine waiting at the entrance to the courtyard.

Mr. Tortoni could see he didn't have much choice. He walked to the car, trying hard to hold his head high.

"*Ciao!*" Nobu called.

"*Arrivederci!*" Leila added.

"I hope they have instant coffee in prison!" Charli shouted.

Everyone laughed, but then the whole group grew quiet. *It's funny*, Leila thought. *I couldn't wait to bust the guy—and now I just feel sorry for him.*

"So, Derek, what about New York next summer?" Jami asked.

Derek Hammond's eyes twinkled. "I have a philosophy," he said. "Never break up a winning team—unless they embezzle and steal. I want every one of you in New York next summer!"

All the interns cheered.

Then Mr. Hammond turned to Jami and pulled her close. "You, I want all year." He leaned in close to kiss her.

Leila sighed. Was Rome the most romantic city in the world, or what?

Charli turned to Paolo. "So are you coming to New York, too?" she asked.

He nodded. "Of course," he said. "I will check out the pizza and pasta. Get some ideas." He leaned in and kissed her softly.

Ryan came up beside Leila. "So we'll hang out together when you're in New York, right?" he said with a wink.

"No," Leila said.

Ryan's face fell.

"We'll work together," Leila said. Then she winked back.

Ryan wrapped her in his arms. "You know what they say," he told her. "'When in Rome...do as the Romans do....'" He leaned in for a kiss.

"Umm, I think a hug will do just fine," Leila said, smiling.

Ryan grinned. "All right, all right," he said.

Leila looked around at her new friends. She had a feeling she was going to have a great time next summer!

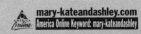

Reading Checklist

andashley

single book!

- ❏ Two's a Crowd
- ❏ Let's Party!
- ❏ Calling All Boys
- ❏ Winner Take All
- ❏ P. S. Wish You Were Here
- ❏ The Cool Club
- ❏ War of the Wardrobes
- ❏ Bye-Bye Boyfriend
- ❏ It's Snow Problem
- ❏ Likes Me, Likes Me Not
- ❏ Shore Thing
- ❏ Two for the Road
- ❏ Surprise, Surprise!
- ❏ Sealed With A Kiss
- ❏ Now You See Him, Now You Don't
- ❏ April Fools' Rules!
- ❏ Island Girls
- ❏ Surf, Sand, and Secrets
- ❏ Closer Than Ever
- ❏ The Perfect Gift

so little time

- ❏ How to Train a Boy
- ❏ Instant Boyfriend
- ❏ Too Good To Be True
- ❏ Just Between Us
- ❏ Tell Me About It
- ❏ Secret Crush

Mary-Kate and Ashley Sweet 16

- ❏ Never Been Kissed
- ❏ Wishes and Dreams
- ❏ The Perfect Summer
- ❏ Getting There
- ❏ Starring You and Me
- ❏ My Best Friend's Boyfriend

MARY-KATE AND ASHLEY in ACTION!

- ❏ Makeup Shake-up
- ❏ The Dream Team

Super Specials:

- ❏ My Mary-Kate & Ashley Diary
- ❏ Our Story
- ❏ Passport to Paris Scrapbook
- ❏ Be My Valentine

**Available wherever books are sold, or
call 1-800-331-3761 to order.**

Mary-Kate and Ashley's

New York Times Bestselling Book Series!

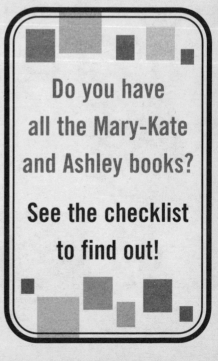